# Happy Birthday, Mama!

### By Bonnie Pryor
### Illustrated by Carolyn Bracken

A Next Step Book™ / Little Helpers™
A LITTLE SIMON BOOK
Published by Simon & Schuster, Inc.

"Why are you cooking and cooking?" asked Robert.

"Today is Mama's birthday," said Daddy. "I am fixing her favorite dinner."

"And a birthday cake?"

"That is a good idea," said Daddy.
"Would you like to help me make it?"

Robert washed his hands,

and Daddy got him a chair to stand on.

Then Daddy got butter, sugar, eggs, and flour.

"Can I pour?" asked Robert.

"Yes," said Daddy. "But first I must read the recipe. It will tell us how much of everything we need."

Daddy measured carefully, and Robert poured everything into a bowl.

"I'll crack the eggs," said Robert. "OOPS!"

Daddy picked all of the egg shells out of the batter.

"What's this stuff?" asked Robert.
"Baking powder," Daddy answered. "It
will make the cake puff up."

Daddy poured the batter into the pans
and put them in the oven.

Robert watched through the window
in the oven door. Soon the cake was a
golden brown.

"Now what do we do?"

"Now we let the cake cool while we get nice and clean for Mama. Then we will frost the cake."

Daddy helped Robert put on his blue pants and new striped shirt.

"Will Mama like this shirt?" asked Robert.

"She will love it," said Daddy. "Oh, dear. I forgot to wrap Mama's present."

"Can I help?" asked Robert.

"Yes, but don't tell. It's a secret," said Daddy.

"I like secrets."

"Me, too," said Daddy.

Robert held the paper so Daddy could put on the tape. Then he put on a big red bow.

Daddy put frosting on the sides of the cake. Robert frosted the top.

"How shall we decorate the cake?" asked Daddy.

"With robots," said Robert. "I think Mama will like robots."

Daddy drew a robot with frosting
while Robert licked the bowl.

"There, we are all ready,"
said Daddy. "Oh, no!"

Daddy washed Robert's face and
hands. Just then they heard Mama
coming to the door.

"Are you ready?" asked Daddy.

"Ready," said Robert.